THE GRUNT AND THE GROUCH

Beastly Feast!

TRACEY CORDEROY

ILLUSTRATED BY
LEE WILDISH

Stripes

LOOK OUT FOR:

CONTENTS

CHAPTER ONE

Rummmmble! The Grunt stuck his head into the fridge, peered around and groaned. It was bare from top to bottom. They were all out of mouldy cheese, hairy cakes and cockroach delight. And Grouchy had nabbed the last piece of plughole-hair pie!

Grunty's tummy gave another rumble – he was *starving*.

"*Grouchy!*" he bellowed, his head still stuffed in the fridge. "Come 'ere!"

The Grouch pattered into the kitchen.
"Oh no – you're stuck!" cried the small
green troll. "Don't panic, I'll rescue you!"

He sank his nails into Grunty's
bottom and started to tug
like mad.

"*Geroff!*" growled The Grunt. "I'm *not* stuck!" He shot a hairy, purple arm behind his back, pushed Grouchy away and backed out of the fridge.

"Why haven't you done the shopping?" he bellowed.

"It was *your* turn," said Grouchy.

"Wasn't!"

"Was!"

"Wasn't!"

"Was!" cried The Grouch. "You told me last week that if I untidied the wardrobe and remembered *not* to flush the toilet, you'd do the shopping. So, see – it *was* your turn!"

Just then, the letter box clicked open and an envelope sailed through and landed on the floor.

9

"*Humph!*" snorted Grunty. "I bet that's just another bill! No food in the house and a big fat bill to pay. What a day this is turning into!"

He stomped across to the front door, snatched up the letter and was about to rip it up when…

"Wait!" cried Grouchy. "On the back – it's us! *Look!*"

The Grunt flipped over the envelope. Somebody had drawn a picture of them!

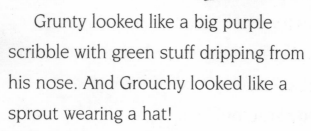

Grunty looked like a big purple scribble with green stuff dripping from his nose. And Grouchy looked like a sprout wearing a hat!

GRUNT AND GROUCH

"They look *just* like us, don't they?" beamed Grouchy.

"Yeah, but who could have sent it?" asked The Grunt.

He tore open the envelope. Inside was a letter and two posh-looking tickets. Grunty unfolded the letter and started to read.

It was from Fred, a boy they'd met when they'd been teachers for a day at Sparkleton Primary – the most spotless school in the world. (Although it had never been quite the same after the trolls' Rats Awards!)

"Hey, listen to this!" cried Grunty. "Fred says there's a posh party at school *this afternoon!*"

He read on…

11

"The school's won some healthy food award! The Mayoress will be there … and there's going to be *tons* of grub! Fred's parents have got chickenpox and can't go, so we can have their tickets instead!"

He waved two silver tickets under Grouchy's nose.

Mr Spickspan cordially invites you to
High Tea
to celebrate Sparkleton Primary's
Healthy Food Award.

Date and time: 15th July – 3.15 for 4p.m.
Venue: The school hall
Dress: Smart

"But look," groaned Grouchy, "the invite says that tea's going to be 'high' so how am *I* meant to reach it? And won't it all be *healthy*, too? Yuck!"

"Never mind that!" cried Grunty. "I'll think of something. At least we're gonna get some grub – and without even going shopping! Come on, let's get ready."

They darted upstairs to get changed. The invite said that they had to look smart, but they didn't own any nice clothes.

"I bagsy the bathroom rug for a cloak!" cried Grunty.

"Only if I can have the bedroom lampshade for a hat!" tittered The Grouch.

CHAPTER TWO

At ten past three, the trolls arrived at the school gates. They gaped at the line of posh parents making their way inside.

"Look at their big silly hats!" giggled Grouchy.

"Ridiculous!" growled Grunty. "Come on, follow me."

Tummies rumbling loudly, they made their way across the playground and joined the back of the queue. The peep-squeak man in front glanced over

his shoulder. When he saw Grouchy's
lampshade hat, his mouth dropped
open in surprise. He nudged his wife
and as she turned to look, the feather
in her hat tickled Grunty's nose.

"Now look what you've done!" the
peep-squeak lady shrieked. "Disgusting!"

"What?" Grunty shrugged. "It was just a sneeze."

Suddenly, a pair of shiny black shoes came squeaking down the line. They stopped before the trolls and their owner gave a horrified gasp.

"Not *you* two!" hissed the head teacher, straightening his already straight tie. Mr Spickspan hadn't forgiven the trolls for the time they'd ruined his RATS Awards and almost wrecked his school.

"*You* haven't been invited! Please leave!"

"What are *these* then?" growled Grunty. He fumbled inside his cloak and pulled out two crumpled tickets.

"So nah nah nah nah nah!" giggled The Grouch, blowing a giant raspberry.

As several parents tutted, Mr
Spickspan's left eye gave a nervous
twitch. He didn't want a scene. Not
today. There was a reporter coming from
the local newspaper. He could see the
headline now…

TROLL TROUBLE at
Sparkleton Primary - *again!*

"All right!" he hissed. "But I'll be watching you, so don't do … *anything!*"

"As if we would!" The Grunt smiled. "Come on, Grouchy!"

They legged it down the length of the queue and hurried into the hall. "Right!" cried Grunty. "Where's the grub? I'm *starving!*"

"I can't *see!*" moaned Grouchy, bouncing up and down. "Grunty, I'm too small – lift me up!"

Grunty scooped him up and plonked him on top of his head. As he carried on searching for the food, Grouchy found himself looking down on all the fancy hats. It was far too tempting just to sit there. Quick as a flash, he swapped a few things around, then added some finishing touches of his own – mostly green and slimy!

He was almost done when a hat appeared with a bunch of shiny cherries on top. Normally Grouchy wouldn't eat cherries – they were *way* too healthy – but today he was *starving*, so he plucked one off, bit into it and…

"OWWWW!" he yelled.

It was a *fake*!

He tossed it away with half his tooth still buried inside. It landed with a *plop!* in Mr Spickspan's glass of fruit punch.

"Uh oh!" gasped Grouchy, as the furious head teacher stomped towards them. "Quick, Grunty, leg it!"

Grunty whisked Grouchy off his head and they sprinted through the crowd. They hadn't gone far when they bumped into Fred and his friends, Lottie and Billy, who were busy taking people's coats.

"Fred," puffed Grunty, "where's the grub?"

"In the kitchen," whispered Fred. "But you won't like it. It's all healthy and boring, thanks to Mrs Boil."

"Never mind that!" cried Grunty. "Lead us to it!"

CHAPTER THREE

As they reached the kitchen, Grunty skidded to a halt. "Where's Mrs Boil?" he whispered.

Lottie smiled. "You don't need to worry about *her*. She'll be busy serving drinks in the hall all afternoon!"

The trolls looked around the spotless kitchen and gasped in disbelief. Healthy food was sat on fancy china plates on top of the shiny worktops. Grunty shook his head. He'd never seen so many vegetables!

"Yuck!" he groaned, untying his cloak and dumping it on the floor. "I might be starving but I'm not eating *that!*"

"Me neither!" sighed Grouchy, tossing down his lampshade hat. "So what are we going to do?"

Grunty scratched his head thoughtfully. Suddenly it came to him. "Quick – search the cupboards!" he cried.

Everyone darted to the cupboards and pulled open the doors. "Hang on," said Billy, "what are we searching *for*?"

"Anything to make this food taste nice!" cried Grunty.

In no time at all, a selection of "goodies" were lined up on the table – ketchup, mustard, vinegar, curry paste and a giant jar of pickled onions.

Grunty leaned across and snatched up a bowl of celery dip.

Right! Let's get started!

"Add some mustard!" Grouchy cried excitedly. He opened the jar of thick yellow mustard and Grunty scooped out a huge handful.

He plopped it into the celery dip, gave it a nice big stir, then slurped the rest off his hairy fingers. "Delicious!" He grinned. "Right, what's next?"

One by one, each boring plate of food was made more "delicious".

Fred spiced up the dull cucumber sandwiches with lashings of curry paste, while Lottie drenched the apple-crisps in vinegar.

Billy dive-bombed the yoghurt surprise with handfuls of pickled onions.

24

Grunty smiled. "Now *those* will be a lovely surprise!"

Finally, Grouchy iced the fruit and fibre fairy cakes with nice big dollops of ketchup. Then everyone stood back to admire their work.

Grunty's stomach rumbled loudly. "I'm sure Mrs Boil won't mind if we just have a taste," he said. He picked up a couple of sandwiches and passed the plate to Grouchy.

"Mmmm!" he cried, his mouth full. "Everyone's going to *love* this grub!"

"Yeah." Grouchy dribbled. "*Trollific!*"

Suddenly, Grunty spotted something perched on top of the fridge. "Ah ha!" he cried, stomping over. "What's *this*?"

25

"That's Mrs Boil's special carrot cake for when the Mayoress makes her speech," said Lottie. "They're going to light those two sparklers on top!"

Grunty's gaze wandered from the carrot cake to a box beside it. On the lid, in big black letters, were the words:

DO NOT TOUCH!

"Hmmm…" said Grunty thoughtfully, squeezing a spot on his chin. He tore off the lid and his beetle-black eyes grew wide. It was *packed* with sparklers!

He grabbed two enormous handfuls, and stuffed them *all* into the cake.

Then Grouchy stuck in some sausages on sticks to make it *extra* pretty!

They'd only just finished when a

group of children burst into the kitchen to collect the food.

"Just in time!" said Grunty. "Here it is!"

"There's a special stand for that cake," said Fred. "It's behind the curtain on the stage. I'm meant to take it there."

"I'll do that!" Grunty smiled. "We don't want anyone seeing it before the big moment or it'll spoil the surprise!"

He scooped up the cake and gazed at the sparklers.

Sparkleton's gonna really sparkle now!

CHAPTER FOUR

The trolls hurried out of the kitchen and made their way backstage. Grouchy stood guard as Grunty popped the cake on its stand.

"Done," he whispered, appearing at Grouchy's side. "Now let's tuck in! I'm starving!"

As the children handed around the nibbles, the trolls grabbed handfuls. They ate and ate, but *still* there was more. Why was nothing running out?

Grunty peered around and spied the Mayoress toss her fruit and ketchup fairy cake on to the brim of a posh lady's hat. He nudged The Grouch. "See that?" He scowled. "After all your hard work!"

Parents were complaining too. The trolls could hardly believe their ears!

"Urrgh!" groaned a peep-squeak man.

"Apples and *vinegar* – disgusting!"

"And don't touch that celery dip!" whispered another. "It's *vile!*"

29

"Yeuch!" heaved Fred's teacher, Mr Smart. He spat out two pickled onions and stared at his yoghurt surprise.

"'Ere – have this," growled Grunty, handing him a sick bag. "Just in case…"

Mr Spickspan nibbled a corner off a cucumber sandwich and started to cough like mad. "W-water!" he spluttered. He thrust his head into the bowl of fruit punch and was lapping it up like a dog when *click!* went the reporter's camera!

By the time the trolls were stuffed to bursting, everyone else looked close to being sick!

Mrs Boil stared in horror. Someone had tampered with her healthy nibbles! And she knew exactly who it was … those trolls!

She was about to go and sort them out when the Mayoress staggered on to the stage. It was time for her speech and the unveiling of the cake. The Mayoress gave a small smile and put her hanky to her mouth – she couldn't remember the last time she'd felt so sick! She swallowed hard. "Ladies and gentlemen…" she began. "I would like to congratulate Sparkleton Primary for winning this *healthy* food award. It has been a …

31

um … *lovely* party! Mrs Boil must take all the credit for the disgust— I mean, *delicious* food, and I'd like to invite her on to the stage to unveil her … um … masterpiece."

Stifling a burp, she nodded at Mrs Boil, who crept on to the stage. If those trolls had ruined her nibbles, what had they done to her *cake*?

Nervously, she pulled a cord and the curtains opened. There was her carrot cake, covered in sausages and hundreds of sparklers! It was ruined.

Hands trembling, she struck a match and lit just one.

"Hooray!" cheered Grunty, as sparks from the sparkler began to light the rest.

"Woo hooo!" Grouchy clapped. "It's glowing like a rocket!"

The trolls beamed. But why was everyone backing away? Suddenly…

BOOOOM!

"*No!*" wailed Mrs Boil, as sticky carrot cake rained down, splattering everyone in crumbs and bits of sausage. "I'll have you trolls for this!"

"Time to go!" cried Grouchy, legging it towards the door.

"Wait for me!" panted Grunty, thumping behind.

They zipped past Mr Spickspan slumped in a chair, just as the reporter zoomed in for a close-up.

Don't forget to say cheese!

No! Cheesy meatballs and custard!

CHAPTER ONE

Whoosh…

"Grunty, Grunty!" panted The Grouch, racing into the kitchen. He tugged Grunty's arm. "Have you remembered what day it is?"

The Grunt was making hairy cakes. He licked the spoon thoughtfully and stared at The Grouch. He was clutching a scruffy drawing in his hand. Grunty scratched his head. Then suddenly it came to him…

It was *Halloween* and – oh no – he'd forgotten to plan his costume! *Bother*, it looked like Grouchy had remembered. Now he'd boast…

"Ha ha!" beamed The Grouch, waving the drawing. "This is my Halloween costume! I'm just off to make it, then *I'll* be ready to go trick or treating!"

"Give us a look then," said Grunty.

"Nope!" smiled The Grouch. "You'll copy."

He stuffed the drawing under his hat and raced off to the goodies shelf. He'd get all the best bits now – the biggest bogeys, the slimiest snot, the jarful of plughole hair! He knew exactly what he needed…

"*I want that,*" said The Grunt, sneaking up behind The Grouch and swiping a jar of bogeys from his hand.

"Give 'em back!" yelled Grouchy. "I need them for my costume!"

"Me too," said The Grunt.

"No you don't – copycat!" cried Grouchy. "You don't even know what your costume *is* yet!"

"Yes I do!" growled The Grunt. "So there!"

The Grouch snatched up a bottle of snot, but Grunty swiped it off him. "I need that too," he growled, "for *my* costume!"

Grouchy stamped his tiny foot. "You're spoiling everything!" He scowled. "How can I be a bogey-monster-with-extra-drippy-slimy-snot-and-a-plughole-hair-moustache, when you've nicked the bogeys, the snot *and* the plug—"

Suddenly, Grouchy stopped. He and Grunty stared at the goodies shelf. The

40

plughole hair was there for the taking…

In a flash, they made a dive for it, but Grunty got there first.

"Fine!" scowled Grouchy. "Be a meanie then! I'll make a different costume. And it'll be even better. Yeah, I know, I'm gonna be a … were-troll!"

Suddenly, a dreamy look crept over Grunty's face. *A were-troll!* Wow! That was brilliant! But if anyone was cut out to be a were-troll, it was *him*. Were-trolls were big. Were-trolls were hairy. Were-trolls were mean and grumpy! Grouchy was just small and green and warty!

"*Here*," said The Grunt, "'ave the bogeys back – *I'm* gonna be the were-troll! You can 'ave the bottle of snot back too."

"OK," said Grouchy, trying his best not to sound too pleased. His plan to trick The Grunt had worked! Now *he* could be the bogey monster, just like he'd planned, except...

"Please may I have the plughole hair too?" Grouchy asked politely. "I need it for my plughole-hair moustache."

"No!" snapped The Grunt. "I need this hair for my hairy were-troll costume!"

He thundered away clutching the jar of plughole hair. He needed every single strand. In fact, now he came to think of it, one measly jar of plughole hair

42

wouldn't make a *whole* were-troll
costume! He'd have to go on a hair-hunt.
Now where should he start...?

CHAPTER
TWO

Two hours later, Grunty stomped into the bathroom. He'd searched everywhere he could think of for hair, but he still didn't have nearly enough to make his costume.

He climbed into the filthy bath, stuffed his fingers down the plughole and wiggled them around a bit. Hang on, there *was* something down there! Carefully, Grunty pulled it out…

"*Bother!*" he roared, as a fat, hairy spider wriggled between his fingers.

He heaved himself up and was about to climb out when something burst through the door. It looked like a big, slimy pea wearing a hat.

"*Rahhhhh!*" cried The Grouch. "The bogey monster's coming to get you!"

Grunty sighed.

"What's wrong?" asked Grouchy. "Wait
– where's your costume?"

"I can't find enough hair!" groaned
Grunty. "I can't
come trick
or treating
tonight."

Grouchy looked sad. "But we *always* go together! There must be somewhere we can get some hair."

Suddenly… "Wait!" he cried. "How about the hairdressers?"

"Oh yeah!" gasped Grunty. "There's always piles on the floor! Well, what are we waiting for? Let's go!"

They raced downstairs. "Hang on," said Grunty. He grabbed a dirty saucepan from the kitchen. "We can collect the hair in this!" He darted out of the house with Grouchy squelching behind. "Hurry up or we'll miss the bus!" he cried.

"I can't!" puffed The Grouch. "It's this snot! I'm sticking to the pavement!"

The three-thirty bus was about to pull off as the trolls leaped aboard. "Hold on," said the bus driver, scowling at Grouchy. "No slimy *things* are allowed on my seats."

The Grouch beamed. "I'm a bogey mon—"

"He'll sit on my lap!" Grunty cut in. He scooped up Grouchy and dived for a seat.

The bus pulled off. Grouchy smiled. Sitting up on Grunty's lap meant he could see for once, and he and Grunty spent the whole journey secretly flicking bogeys at the passengers!

Fifteen minutes later, the bus stopped on the high street, right outside Claude's, the hairdressing salon.

"I like being a bogey monster!" said Grouchy, as they stepped off the bus. He flicked some snot at a passer-by. "It's fun!"

Grunty peered through the salon window. It looked very posh. "Yuck," he groaned. "It's *horrible*."

"*Revolting!*" shuddered Grouchy.

A peep-squeak lady was sipping tea as a hairdresser man cut her hair. He jumped in surprise to see two snotty noses pressed against the glass, and *snip!* went his shiny scissors before he could stop them. A huge chunk of the lady's hair tumbled to the floor. Grunty's eyes lit up. He'd have that bit!

"Come on!" he cried, hurrying to the door. As he pushed it open, he noticed a sign on the glass.

Feeling blue?
Need a free hairdo?
Let Claude work his magic on you!
Models needed NOW!

"They can forget *that!*" growled The Grunt, stomping into the salon. "Nobody's touching *my* hair…"

CHAPTER THREE

The hairdresser man left the peep-squeak lady still sipping her tea and flounced across the salon to the trolls.

He was wearing a frilly shirt and smelled of sickly-sweet shampoo. His long, swishy fringe fell over one eye. He swept it back and smiled at his reflection as he passed a sparkly mirror.

"Good afternoon, gentlemen. I'm Claude – Hairdresser to the Stars!" he gushed. "How can I hel—" Suddenly,

53

Claude stopped and gaped at the trolls. One of them was covered in *slime*.

He snatched up a newspaper and popped it on the floor. "Could sir please stand on this?" he said.

Grouchy squelched forward and stood on it. "There!" twinkled Claude. "That's better! But – my goodness – you *do* need my magic, don't you?"

"No!" snapped The Grunt. "We *don't* need our hair done, if that's what you mean!"

"We just need some hair, thanks!" Grouchy added nervously. He dropped to his knees and started scooping up hair from the floor. It stuck to his hands, which were still covered in snot.

A salon full of peep-squeaks watched in horror. If anyone needed a makeover, it was these two! Especially the purple one – *such* a last-season colour!

"Hold on a *teensy* moment!" sang Claude. "You can't just *take* that hair. No, no, no! I need models and you two are *perfect*. There's so much I could try out! Then, when I've worked my magic, you can have as much hair as you like!"

When Grouchy heard this, he shot
off the floor and hid behind The Grunt.
"Quick, let's hop it," he whispered.
"I don't want to be a—"

"Not so fast," hissed Grunty, taking
The Grouch aside. "If we leave now, I
won't have a costume! I thought you
wanted me to go trick or treating
tonight!"

"I do," sniffed
Grouchy. "But I'm
not being a
model! They'll
wash my
bogey
costume
down the
plughole!"

Grunty sighed. Grouchy was right. And that meant one thing. *He'd* have to be Claude's model!

"Right," he whispered. "Listen up – I've got a plan…"

When Grunty had finished whispering his plan, Grouchy looked confused. "So *you* get prettied up," he said, "and while Claude's working his magic, *I* swipe hair off the floor?"

"No!" hissed Grunty. "I DON'T get prettied up! *I* keep Claude talking about what he's going to do while *you* creep around collecting hair. Then we both hop it before he gets started. Got it?"

"Er … got it!" said Grouchy. "I think…"

Grunty turned back to Claude. "All right," he growled. "I'll be your model!"

"Lovely!" cried Claude, clapping his hands. "I'll just finish off my lady first."

"Fine," said Grunty, "but I've got *tons* of questions to ask before you touch a hair…"

"Of course!" beamed Claude. He led The Grunt towards the sparkly mirrors, helped him into a long black gown and settled him on a swivelly chair.

Meanwhile, Grouchy had sat himself down in the waiting area. It wasn't time to swipe the hair yet. Grunty had told him to wait until Claude was busy chatting.

He picked up a magazine to look at while he waited. As he did, something fell to the floor. He snatched it up and suddenly his eyes grew wide. It was his favourite comic. The very latest one!

"Wow!" he gasped, making himself comfy.

CHAPTER FOUR

In no time at all, Claude's peep-squeak
lady left the salon twinkling. "Now…"
Claude beamed at Grunty, "your turn!"

Grunty gulped. Would Grouchy
remember the plan? He could see
Grouchy's reflection in the mirror and
he didn't seem to be paying much
attention!

"Tell me what you're gonna do first,"
growled Grunty. "*Everything…*"

Claude smiled and started raking his

fingers through Grunty's knotty hair.

"Dear me," he sighed, shaking his head.

Next, he started to rattle off a list of
what he had planned – washing, cutting,
dyeing, drying, curling, fluffing-up. Grunty
squirmed. Fluffing-up sounded like
torture!

On and on Claude droned. The salon
was hot and stuffy. *Buzzzzzz* went the
hairdryers. *Sssssssss* went the taps. On
and on and on…

Soon, Grunty's eyes began to feel
heavy. Then slowly, *very* slowly … they
closed.

Meanwhile, Grouchy was in the middle of
an *awesome* "Splat Bat" story! This week's

Mega Monster Mag was wicked! The Vampire Splat Bats had teamed up with Blaa the Bogey Monster! Captain Sparkle had *no* chance now…

The minutes whizzed by as Grouchy read on … one more story … then another one. Suddenly, he heard a familiar sound…

Zzzzz … zzzzz… Grouchy froze. Was that Grunty snoring? No – it *couldn't* be! He'd only, just this minute, sat down. Hadn't he?

Nervously, Grouchy looked up and checked the clock on the wall. Five o'clock – he'd been reading for an *hour*!

He tossed away the comic and threw himself on to the floor. *Hair* – he needed hair, right now! Then he'd have to rescue

Grunty before Claude started
working his magic!

He scrabbled around
scooping up hair. There
seemed to be *tons*
on the floor.
Tons and tons
of … *purple* hair.
Trembling,
Grouchy got to his
feet and peered up at the snoring Grunty.
"Uh oh!" he gulped. Claude had worked
his magic *already*…

Grunty's hair was now black and fluffy
with a big white stripe down the middle!
He was going to be *furious*.

"Grunty! Wake up!" yelled The Grouch,
aiming a curler at him.

Oh no!

63

"Excuse me – I haven't
finished yet!" flapped Claude.

Grouchy ignored him and gave The
Grunt a sharp nip on the ankle. Suddenly,
Grunty began to stir.

Quick as a flash, Grouchy swivelled
Grunty's chair around so that he had his
back to the mirror. If he saw himself now
there'd be *big* trouble!

"*Wha!*" snorted Grunty, rubbing his eyes.

"RUN!" yelled Grouchy. He grabbed Grunty's arm and tugged him towards the door. Peep-squeaks gasped as they thundered past. The big one looked *terrifying*!

"Did you get the hair?" cried Grunty when they got outside. But Grouchy just kept on running.

"Err – a bit," he puffed.

Then suddenly…

"*Arrgghhh!*" cried a peep-squeak lady pointing at The Grunt.

M-m-monster!

Everybody run!

The street cleared in seconds. What was going on? Puzzled, Grunty looked down at himself. He was still wearing the long black gown, but surely it couldn't be that? He felt his hair. His *hair* – what *had* Claude done?

He thundered across to a shop window and peered at his reflection. His jaw dropped – he looked like a giant skunk! It was wicked! And it was *super-scary*!

Just then, the moon began to shine. It was time to go trick or treating!

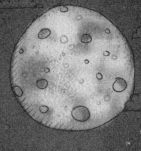

CHAPTER ONE

Prod... "Move!" cried Grunty. But Snail didn't even twitch!

The trolls were in the garden, racing their pets, but so far they'd barely stirred.

"That makes Slug the winner!" Grouchy beamed.

Grunty peered down at Slug. "How come? *He* hasn't moved either!"

"He *has*!" cried Grouchy, pointing out a *teeny* slithery trail. "See – there! So hand over my bogey winnings!"

Grunty shook his head and clung on to the bogey jar. "These pets are *useless!*" he roared. "They don't do anything!"

He threw a stick. "Fetch, Snail!" he commanded. But Snail didn't budge. Grunty picked him up and peered into his shell. "Now where have you gone?" he bellowed. He shook his head and sighed. "Grouchy, I think it's time we got a new pet."

Grouchy gave a horrified gasp and covered Slug's ears. (He wasn't sure if Slug *had* ears, so he covered the bits where ears would be if he had any.) "Don't say that!" he whispered. "You'll upset him!"

But even Grouchy had to admit that Slug was a bit boring. He didn't have fleas. He didn't chase the postman. *Or* chew holes in the curtains. And he hardly *ever* burped out loud!

For the next half an hour, Grunty and Grouchy sat side by side in the mud, arguing about whether they should get a new pet or not. Eventually, they decided that they would.

"Right," growled The Grunt, "now that's settled, what pet shall we get?"

GRUNT AND THE GROUCH

"Something with fleas!" cried Grouchy. "And something that pongs and has tons of hair and loves mud and rubbish!"

"Hmmm…" said Grunty, picking his nose and licking his fat, hairy finger. "Like what?"

"I know!" cried Grouchy. "Let's get a gorilla!" He puffed out his cheeks and beat his chest.

"Don't be stupid!" cried Grunty. "A gorilla would eat us out of house and home! We need something smaller. Er, let's see … how about a bat?"

"Bats sleep all day!" groaned Grouchy.

72

"That's no good." He scratched his head.
Choosing a pet was tricky.

"Giraffe!" cried Grouchy.

"Toad!" cried Grunty.

"Orang-utan!"

"Warthog!"

"Hippopotamus!"

On and on they argued. Then finally, Grunty had a great idea.

"Why don't we go to the pet shop?" he said. "We might see something we both like there."

"Good idea!" cried Grouchy excitedly.

Leaving Slug and Snail to entertain themselves, the trolls raced off to the bus stop and caught a bus to town. On the way, they talked about what pets they might find in the pet shop.

And by the time they arrived, they'd agreed on what they wanted. They couldn't believe they hadn't thought of it before!

"Good morning!" called Grouchy, as they hurried into the pet shop. The pet-shop man backed away nervously at the

sight of the trolls. He didn't want them
bringing fleas into his shop!

"We've come to get a new pet,"
grunted Grunty.

Got any
smelly
rats?

CHAPTER TWO

"Wh-what?" gulped the pet-shop man. "You want a smelly rat? But all *my* rats are clean and very clever!"

"Huh! That's no good!" groaned The Grunt. "What else have you got?"

"Anything with fangs that burps a lot?" asked Grouchy.

"How about a rabbit?" suggested the pet-shop man. "These little fellows are so sweet!" He opened the door of the rabbit pen and the trolls peered inside.

"*Yeuch!*" heaved Grouchy.

"They're *fluffy!*" Grunty shuddered.

The man shut the pen door and the trolls took a look around the shop. All these pets looked *way* too clean! None of them were even scratching!

"They all look dead bored," growled Grunty. "You should let them play together."

"NO!" bellowed the pet-shop man, as The Grunt opened the rabbit pen and a herd of fluffy bunnies bounced out. The pet-shop man tried to catch them, but they were just too springy!

Meanwhile, Grouchy had opened the parrots' cage. "*Ta daa!*" he beamed, as they flew out into the shop.

"Now for them spotless rats!"

cried Grunty, opening the rats' cage.

"Please – no!" wailed the pet-shop man. "They'll … they'll … get *dirty*!" But it was too late. The rats were out and scurrying across the floor. Then *splat, splat, splat* – parrot poo rained down through the air…

"GET OUT!" yelled the pet-shop man. "NOW!"

The trolls made their way to the door. "You want to get some *interesting* pets!" cried Grouchy.

"With fleas!" added Grunty. And he slammed the door behind him.

Out on the pavement, Grouchy looked upset. He'd been sure they'd find a nice new pet in there. "What are we going to do *now*?" he said. But, for once, Grunty didn't have an answer.

They wandered back through the park and Grunty jumped in all the muddy puddles. But, try as he might, he couldn't cheer Grouchy up.

"Look, there's an ice-cream van," said Grunty, hurrying over. "You *love* ice cream! Just wait there. I'll even ask if they've got bogey sprinkles!"

Grouchy sat under a
nearby tree and gave a big sigh.
He'd been looking forward to getting
a new pet *so* much.

As he waited, a dog appeared. He was
big and scruffy and brown, and as hairy
as a woolly mammoth! He sniffed the tree
where Grouchy sat. Then he sniffed The
Grouch. He seemed to like Grouchy's
smell because he didn't run away.
Instead, he flopped down
next to him and scratched.

"Wow!" cried Grouchy. "You've got *fleas!*" The dog started to pant. His breath smelled like pongy pond water!

"Here you go, Grouchy!" said The Grunt, stomping back with two ice creams. The fleabaggy dog sprang up and nicked one out of his hand.

"Oi!" cried Grunty, snatching it back.

"Never mind that." The Grouch giggled. "He's got fleas, pongy breath, he's naughty and it looks like he doesn't have a home. He's our perfect pet!"

CHAPTER THREE

Over the next few weeks, the fleabaggy dog (who Grouchy named Grotbag) proved to be the best pet in the world.

Grotbag slurped. Grotbag burped. Grotbag barked at the postman. Grotbag chewed huge holes in the curtains and rolled in muddy puddles wherever he found them.

Dribbling was another of Grotbag's special talents. In just three weeks, the trolls had managed to collect seven jarfuls.

Their goodies shelf had never held so many treats!

And so life went on happily, until one sunny afternoon, when everything changed. The trolls and Grotbag were out in town when Grotbag came nose to nose with … the most *beautiful* dog in the *world*!

She had a curly white coat and a tail like a snowball on a stick. Grotbag had never seen anything so lovely.

As she trotted out of the Pampered
Pooch Parlour, she bumped right into
Grotbag, who was munching on a
crust of stale bread. "Oh, *goodness!*"
shuddered her owner. "What a grubby
dog!"

Gripping her poodle's sparkly lead,
she edged past the trolls. "Don't look at
them, Fifi-Belle, darling!"

Grotbag gazed at the pretty poodle
and his dribbly jaw dropped. A warm,
fuzzy look crept into his eyes. "*Ahhh…*"
he sighed dreamily.

Grunty and Grouchy gaped at each
other. What was wrong with *him*? As Fifi-
Belle was led away, Grotbag scrambled
to his feet and bounded after her…
Grotbag was *in love*!

"*No!*" yelled Grouchy, racing after him.
But Grotbag was already at Fifi-Belle's
side, panting madly.

"Poo!" cried her owner.

"What smelly breath!
Get him away!"

Grunty thundered up behind them
and scooped Grotbag into his arms.
"Come on, we're going home!" he roared.

86

But as the trolls stomped away,
Grotbag noticed that Fifi-Belle was heading
to the park. Maybe he'd see her there
tomorrow. Maybe she'd like him then…

For the rest of the day,
Grotbag whined and
whimpered. He lay in
his basket and
wouldn't eat or play.

That night, the trolls went to bed
feeling very worried. They'd never seen
Grotbag like this before.

Next morning, Grouchy leaped out of
bed and looked around for Grotbag.

"Where is he?" he gasped. "He's
normally chewing a bone on my bed!"

87

They checked the garden. There were
no new holes. They checked the
curtains. There were no new holes.
Where on earth was Grotbag, and what
was he up to?

"Don't worry," said Grunty. "We'll go
and search around town. He's probably
gone back to them lovely bins! Come on!"

As they hurried out of the door,
Grouchy spotted something. There was a
dog by their gate. "Look!" he gasped.
"It's … wait… Oh no, it isn't."

Grouchy shook his head. *This* dog
wasn't Grotbag. *This* dog looked too
clean and neat – it couldn't be!

"Scram!" yelled Grunty crossly. "Go
on… *Grrr!*" But the neat dog came
trotting towards them…

The trolls stared in disbelief. It *was* Grotbag! But he was *clean*, and his fur was *short* and *shiny*. The trolls shuddered in disgust. He must have been to the Pampered Pooch Parlour to look and smell *this* bad.

"Quick!" whispered Grunty. "Get him inside before anyone sees him!"

"Or *smells* him," spluttered Grouchy. "Bad dog, Grotbag!"

CHAPTER FOUR

For the rest of the morning, Grotbag paced about, pawing the front door. His eyes were sad and his clean tail drooped.

"What does he want?" growled The Grunt.

Grouchy shrugged. "Dunno."

They offered him bogeys. They offered him bones. They offered him bogeys *on* bones! But Grotbag just kept on pawing the door and whining.

90

Finally, Grouchy got the message. "Hang on … I think he wants to go walkies!"

Grotbag's ears pricked up at once and his tail started wagging. That was it! He wanted to go to the park.

"Well, I'm not taking him looking like *that*!" growled Grunty. "I want the old Grotbag back!"

The trolls tried everything to persuade Grotbag to get dirty. Drippy ice cream … a muddy bath … they even offered him a food fight! But Grotbag turned up his clean nose at everything.

"He'll have to wear a disguise then," sighed Grunty. "Or no walkies!" He tossed across an old jumper and hat, which Grouchy helped Grotbag put on.

Grotbag sniffed the jumper and whimpered. It *ponged*, and he didn't want to pong! Not today.

On the way to the park, Grotbag trotted by Grunty's side and edged around all the muddy puddles. "What is *wrong* with that dog?" snapped The Grunt. "I wish he was like he used to be."

By the time they arrived it was raining, so Grotbag hurried under a tree to shelter. And there he sat, peering around, for what seemed like hours.

Then, suddenly, Grotbag's eyes twinkled. He wriggled out of Grunty's old jumper, shook off the hat and raced towards…

"Flippin' Fifi-Belle!" scowled The Grunt. "So *that's* why he went to that pampered pooch place! Grotbag's trying to impress that poodle!"

The trolls watched as Grotbag trotted up to Fifi-Belle's owner and presented her with a spotless paw.

They stared as she took it and patted him on the head. Clearly, she didn't recognize Grotbag from yesterday!

Then they watched in horror as Grotbag and Fifi-Belle began to play with a ball. Not chew it up. Not dribble on it – just *play*.

ALPAS 7-9-18

"I've had enough of this!" growled
Grunty. "Come on, let's go and get him!"

"No, wait!" said Grouchy. He'd
spotted something that just might do
the trick. "Look. Over there."

They watched as a smart black poodle
came trotting along the path. Fifi-Belle
gazed up at him.

He barked a little yappy bark. She
barked back. Then her snowbally tail
began to wag. "*Ahhhh!*" she sighed.
It was love at first bark!

They trotted away through the trees
together, their owners strolling behind.
Grotbag hung his head and whimpered.

"It's OK, Grotbag!" cried Grouchy,
dashing over and giving him a hug.
"Forget Fifi-Belle. *We* love you, boy!"

94

The Grunt hurried off and bought
three ice creams. He placed them on the
grass in front of Grotbag.

After a while, Grotbag licked one.
Then he slurped them up, one after the
other, and finished with a giant burp.

"That's more like it!" said Grunty.
"He's back to normal. Let's go home."

They stomped off under the trees and
through the flower beds. Then, as they

MALPAS 7-9-18

reached the park gates, they found a
ginormous puddle!

"Whee!" cried the trolls, jumping in.
"We love muddy puddles!"

"*Woof!*" barked Grotbag, joining them.

Actually – so did he!